Robert and the Sneaker Snobs

by Barbara Seuling
Illustrated by Paul Brewer

A
LITTLE APPLE
PAPERBACK

SCHOLASTIC INC.

New York Toronto London Auckland Sydney
Mexico City New Delhi Hong Kong Buenos Aires

To Laura Tillotson,
who loved Robert at first sight
—B. S.

For Jacqui and Melanie
—P. B.

No part of this publication may be reproduced in whole or in part, or stored in a retrieval system, or transmitted in any form or by any means, electronic, mechanical, photocopying, recording, or otherwise, without written permission of the publisher. For information regarding permission, write to Carus Publishing Company, 315 Fifth Street, Peru, Illinois 61354.

ISBN 0-439-35375-0

All rights reserved. Published by Scholastic Inc., 555 Broadway, New York, NY 10012, by arrangement with Carus Publishing Company. SCHOLASTIC and associated logos are trademarks and/or registered trademarks of Scholastic Inc.

12 11 10 9 8 7 6 5   3 4 5 6/0

Printed in the U.S.A.
First Scholastic printing, January 2002

Contents

The Uncool
Sneakers

Robert thumped upstairs to his room. He flopped into his beanbag chair, yanked off his new sneakers, and threw them across the room. Flo and Billie, his two turtledoves, flapped around in their cage.

All day long, Jesse Meiner had made fun of Robert's new sneakers. "They're so uncool," he said. "Get with it, Robert. Everyone who's cool wears High Jumps."

Robert didn't care if he was cool or not. What difference did it make if he wore his sneakers or High Jumps?

Robert would love to talk to his mom about it. She could always make him feel better. She would say something like, "It's just a lot of silly talk, Rob. Your sneakers are fine." But his mom was at her office on Tuesdays.

Sometimes he could talk to his brother, Charlie, but Charlie liked to tease him, and that's the last thing he needed right now. Besides, Charlie had hockey practice after school, and then he'd probably study with his friend Chris. They were studying the Middle Ages, when battles were fought on horseback and soldiers wore armor and carried banners to show whose army they were in. That's all Charlie talked about these days.

Robert's dad would be home soon. He was a teacher and left school at three o'clock, like Robert did. His dad was harder to talk to. He always liked to make lessons out of problems. Robert wasn't in the mood for a lesson. He had already talked to Paul Felcher, his best friend, on the way home from school. He would just have to wait for his mom to come home.

Robert got up and went to see how his animals were. The birds had calmed down, now that Robert had stopped throwing his shoes around. He opened their cage and let them out for a little exercise.

"Hello, Fuzzy," he said to his pet tarantula. He opened the tank to talk to her. He still didn't handle her much, but he was getting better at it. He was happy just to have her company and to feed her a cricket or two every week.

Tomorrow was Author Day at school. Robert had been looking forward to this day for a long time. Frank Farraday was coming. He was the author of a gazillion books, all about wildlife. That was right up

Robert's alley. He loved animals of all kinds.

Robert filled the little cup in the birdcage with bird food. He refilled the water cup in the bathroom and went back to his room.

"Come on, Flo. Come on, Billie." Robert coaxed the birds down from the curtain rod and onto his arm, then into the cage.

Robert had been thrilled when Mrs. Bernthal chose him to be Frank Farraday's host. That meant he would show the author around and escort him from room to room. But what if Frank Farraday noticed that Robert's sneakers were not High Jumps? Would he care? Would it matter? How could Robert look uncool in front of Frank Farraday?

He had to get his mind off his sneakers. He had a report due on Friday. It had to be about something in the world he didn't like and what he would do to fix it. He dumped his book bag on his bed and took out his notebook and pencil. He sat at his desk and opened the notebook to a new page.

He thought about things he didn't like. Liver. Math. He couldn't write about them.

There would always be liver and math because they were good for you. He just didn't like them.

People making fun of other people really bothered him. What would he do about that? Catch the person and make him apologize. And buy a present for the person that he made fun of so that person would feel better. He tapped his pencil. That was pretty lame.

Smoking. He really hated smoking. It made you look ugly to smoke, and it polluted your lungs and gave you cancer. Once, he and Paul tried to stop people on the street from smoking. His class had just seen a movie about how bad smoking was for you. The people they stopped told them to go away and kept on smoking anyway.

He thought about animals that were treated badly. Robert once saw a picture in a magazine of a fox that had been caught in a steel trap. The fox had chewed its own paw off to get free. Robert's stomach flipped when he thought about it. That would be too hard to think about. He'd better choose something else. But what?

He put his pencil down. He had not written one word. He went downstairs with a soft *thump, thump* to get something to eat. He opened the refrigerator and took out the container of milk. He smelled it. His mom was so busy, she didn't always remember to replace the milk before it went sour.

Good. It was fine. He poured a tall glassful and then found some chocolate-covered jelly cookies to go with it.

It was amazing how cookies and milk always made him feel better. He hadn't thought about sneakers for at least ten minutes.

No Help

As he licked the chocolate coating off a cookie, Robert heard the car in the driveway. Sure enough, the clock on the kitchen wall said it was 3:42 exactly, the time his dad drove into the driveway every day. Robert heard the squeal of the garage door opening and closing and the car door slamming.

"Hi, Tiger," said Robert's dad, coming into the kitchen from the garage entrance.

"Hi, Dad."

"What's cooking?"

"Nothing," said Robert.

"Really?" His dad put his briefcase on the table and helped himself to a juice drink from the refrigerator. "That was your day? Nothing?"

"Well . . ."

"What is it, Tiger? You look worried." He sat down.

"Dad, all the kids are wearing the same kind of sneakers in school. They're called High Jumps."

"And?"

"And my sneakers are not that kind."

"Well, Robert. Didn't your mother just get you those sneakers?"

"Yes, but . . ."

"Well, money doesn't grow on trees, Robert," his dad said with a smile. "We can't get you a new pair of sneakers just so you can be like your friends."

"No, Dad, I . . ."

"Your new sneakers don't hurt your feet, do they?"

"Oh, no. It's not . . ."

"Well, then it would be a waste of money to get another pair for no good reason. Isn't that true?"

"Yes, that's what I . . ."

"Of course. That's right. Wear the sneakers you have and be happy with them. I'm sure your mother would say the same thing." His dad got up and picked up his briefcase. "I'll be in my study grading papers if you need me for anything," he said.

How did that happen? Robert wondered, watching his father leave the kitchen. I didn't want to buy new sneakers. I just wanted to figure out how to stop the kids from teasing me. He never even heard my problem, but he thinks he fixed it!

He just had to face this sneakers thing on his own. Grown-ups were no help.

The Author

Robert took the school bus. He decided to wear his hiking boots from last year, which were a bit too small. His toes felt like they were in jail. He didn't think they would feel any better walking four blocks to school.

When the bus stopped at Paul's corner, Robert opened the window. "Get on the bus, Paul!" he shouted, waving his arm to catch Paul's attention. Paul got on and sat next to Robert.

"How come we're riding?" asked Paul.

They usually walked in good weather so they had more time to talk.

"My boots are tight. I don't think I can walk too far in them."

"So why are you wearing tight boots?" asked Paul. "I thought you just got new sneakers."

"Well," said Robert, "because of Frank Farraday." Robert looked embarrassed. "I don't want him to think I'm uncool."

"Uncool?" said Paul, frowning. "Don't listen to Jesse and the other kids. You're one of the coolest people I know. You have a tarantula for a pet, don't you?"

Paul always knew what to say to make Robert feel better.

"I guess," Robert said. "I was dumb for letting Jesse bother me. But it's too late now." He tried to wiggle his toes and couldn't.

"It's only for today," said Paul.

The minute Robert got into his classroom, he checked everything. All the books by Frank Farraday were on display around the room. A big poster, painted by Paul, the best artist in the class, hung on the door.

Around the edges of the poster were pictures of books with titles printed on them. *Wildlife Rescue. A Bird's Life. Coyotes in the Backyard. Return of the Wolves. Animal Feet. Bringing Back the Buffalo. Gorilla Baby. In Search of Humpback Whales.* Frank Farraday had written lots more, but those were the ones they had in their class library.

Jesse walked up to Robert. His eyes went right to the hiking boots. "Those are cool—" Robert felt his heart jump "—if you're in the country," said Jesse. "What is it with you? Get in step, man!"

"Going hiking, Robert?" asked Joey Rizzo. Abby Ranko and Melissa Thurm giggled. Robert could not think about that now. He went up to Mrs. Bernthal's desk.

"Mrs. Bernthal, may I borrow a pitcher from the teachers' lounge? Mr. Farraday might like a drink of water."

"Yes, you may, Robert. That's a very good idea," said Mrs. Bernthal.

Robert left the room. In the teachers' lounge he took a big plastic pitcher and let the water run into it while he searched for a cup. He returned to his classroom with the pitcher sloshing over with water. Stuffed in his shirt pocket was a plastic cup.

"Oh, dear," said Mrs. Bernthal, moving papers to make room on her desk. Robert put the pitcher down without spilling a drop. He put the plastic cup next to the pitcher.

Robert fidgeted in his seat. He was wearing his favorite green shirt, which was always fine, but today it made him itch. His toes were hot. If only he could take his boots off for a while.

The class was supposed to be following the instructions on pages four and five of their math workbooks. Robert couldn't help looking at the folder he had made to give to the author. FRANK FARRADAY, AUTHOR was spelled out across the front cover in colored markers. Every other letter was green. The letters in between were black. It really looked nice. Inside the folder, several pages of facts about the author's books had been stapled.

"All right, class. Let's go around the room. Andrew, what's the answer to number one?"

Andrew Liskin answered quickly. "Seventy-eight." Of course it was correct. Andy was a whiz at math.

Matt Blakey was next. Mrs. Bernthal continued around the room until she got to Robert. "Robert, what is the answer to number seven?"

"I didn't get that one," he replied.

"Did you get the one before it?"

"Um, no."

"Which ones did you get?"

"I . . . I didn't get any," Robert replied, staring at the empty pages in front of him.

"Well, you can add that to your home-work tonight," said Mrs. Bernthal. "I know you're excited about Frank Farraday's visit. We all are. But that doesn't excuse you from doing your classwork."

Robert felt his cheeks get hot as Mrs. Bernthal went on to Susanne Lee Rodgers.

Extra homework. He would have to work hard to get all his homework done by eight o'clock. Otherwise, he would not be allowed to watch *The Instant Millionaire*. Robert and Paul watched the program every week to see how much money they would win if they were on the show. Paul once got up to $1,000. Robert never got past $400 but he was still trying. You had to know an awful lot about a gazillion dif-ferent topics to be on the show.

At last, Frank Farraday arrived. Mrs. Bernthal welcomed him.

"Thank you for coming, Mr. Farraday," she said. "We have been reading your books and looking forward to your visit. Children, say good morning to Mr. Farraday." She stepped back to let Mr. Farraday stand in front of the room.

"GOOD MORNING, MISTER FARRADAY," all the children said together.

Mr. Farraday laughed. "Good morning, children," he replied. "You have good wake-up voices. I'm really awake now."

Frank Farraday looked like a movie star. Robert wondered if he got his tan working out in the hot sun with wild animals. He wore a plaid shirt with the neck open, a bandanna tied around his neck, and jeans. And on his feet—Robert couldn't believe it—he had on hiking boots!

Smelly Feet

Frank Farraday told the class about the books he wrote. "I always felt bad that wolves were almost extinct in this country," he said.

"Extinct?" Lester Willis called out. "Do they smell bad?" The class giggled.

"No," said the author. "Extinct means gone forever. There were almost none left in any of the states. People had killed them off. They had been exterminated."

"My dad's an exterminator," Matt Blakey said.

"Class," Mrs. Bernthal said, "please remember your manners. Raise your hand if you want to say something."

Mr. Farraday cleared his throat. Robert jumped up to pour a cup of water for him. A lot of it spilled on Mrs. Bernthal's desk. She came running with a bunch of paper towels to mop it up. Meanwhile, Mr. Farraday drank the water Robert handed him. "Thank you," he said to Robert before he continued.

"You can imagine how excited I was when I heard they were bringing wolves back to one of our big national parks. I wrote and asked if I could come out and be part of the project. Lucky for me, they said I could."

After Frank Farraday talked to the class, he answered questions. Mrs. Bernthal told the class to say thank you to Mr. Farraday, and they did, in their usual way.

"THANK YOU, MISTER FARRADAY," they said as he put his hands over his ears and laughed.

As the children were dismissed for lunch, Robert stayed behind. He gave Frank Farraday the folder he had made. Mr. Farraday looked at it and grinned. "Isn't that nice!" he said. "Thank you so much." He asked where the bathroom was, and Robert escorted him there. Robert waited outside. As they walked back to the classroom together, Robert felt his throat tighten up, but he had to say something.

"You're my favorite author in the whole world," he said.

"Thank you, Robert."

"It must be great to know so much that you can write books about it," Robert said. "You are an expert on everything."

"It's the other way around," said the author. "First I want to write about something that interests me. Then I learn about it until I become almost an expert. It's one of the neat things about being a writer. You get to explore subjects that really interest you."

"Like animals," said Robert.

"Yes, exactly."

Robert had not looked at it that way before. Books had always seemed to just be there. It was fun to know that someone like Frank Farraday had to make a book happen.

Robert looked at his watch. "The parents made a special lunch for you," Robert told Mr. Farraday. "I have to take you to the teachers' lounge. It's down the hall."

"That sounds nice. I'm starved. Lead the way."

Robert left Mr. Farraday at the teachers' lounge.

"Aren't you joining us?" Frank Farraday asked.

"Um, no," said Robert. He would have liked to, but he had to take off his boots. His feet were killing him. "I have something I have to do."

As soon as he got back to the empty classroom, Robert took off his boots. His feet felt like they were on fire. Oh, did his feet feel happy as he wiggled his toes and laughed and wiggled them some more!

He took off his socks, too. That was even better. Robert sat in Mrs. Bernthal's chair, stretching his toes. He was about to tear open a Crunchy Lunch Bar that he carried in his book bag for emergencies when the door opened.

"Mr. Farraday!" he said. "What are you doing here?" He hoped that didn't sound rude. "I mean, aren't you supposed to be having lunch?"

"Oh, yes, yes, I am, and it's wonderful. I just remembered something in here that I want to do before I forget it." He found his

briefcase and opened it. Robert grabbed
the Whiff O' Pine room spray that Mrs.
Bernthal kept in the corner. He sprayed his
feet, in case they smelled.

When Mr. Farraday turned around, he
sniffed the air. "I must be homesick," he said,

"because I can almost smell the pine forests of Maine."

"You live in Maine?" asked Robert. He had never been to Maine, but he had heard about it.

"Yup," answered Mr. Farraday. "Not far from the Oceanographic Institute."

"What's that?" asked Robert.

"It's a place where scientists study the ocean. They learn how pollution affects sea animals. This summer I'm going with them to study sea turtles. That's going to be my next book. Sea turtles are disappearing, and the scientists want to know what we can do about it. So do I."

"Wow," said Robert.

Mr. Farraday handed a book to Robert. "Before I go, I want you to have this. Thanks for your help. Now I'd better get back to that lunch or everyone will wonder what happened to me."

"Thanks," said Robert, too stunned to say anything more.

After the door closed, Robert looked at the book carefully. It was a new one, *Arctic Animals*. Inside, he read what Frank Farraday had written to him.

It was tough putting his socks and boots back on, but Robert had to do it. His job wasn't over yet. He had to stick like glue to Frank Farraday in case the author needed him for anything.

After lunch, a TV crew arrived to film Frank Farraday for the local news. The kids were buzzing with excitement. Members of the crew ran around with cameras and lights. Someone patted the sweat off the reporter's face with a tissue, while someone else dragged wires out of people's way. Other people made sure nobody stood between the reporter and the guy with the camcorder.

"Will we be on TV?" asked Lester Willis.

"I don't know," said Mrs. Bernthal.

Suddenly, the reporter held a microphone out to the author and an incredibly bright light went on. As Frank Farraday spoke to the reporter, Robert thought about the inscription in his book and smiled. Frank Farraday, the famous author, had called Robert his friend.

Lemmings

Robert sat on his bed with his feet in a bucket of water. His mom had poured some Forbush's Foot Bath into it to help soothe his burning feet. Fuzzy was scratching in her tank. Flo and Billie were cooing at each other.

He opened his notebook. He had an idea now for his report. Across the top of a new page he wrote:

OCEAN POLLUTION

But what about ocean pollution? He didn't like it, but what would he do to fix it? It should be something about animals. As he sat staring at the words, wiggling his toes in the warm water, he heard his dad calling him.

"Robert. Your school is on the TV news! Come on down and watch."

Robert almost knocked over the bucket as he got up. He ran down the stairs with his feet still dripping. His mom and Charlie had come running, too.

A reporter was talking about Frank Farraday's visit to Robert's school. The camera zoomed in on Frank Farraday with a bunch of kids around him. For a split second, Robert saw himself at Mr. Farraday's side.

"There you are!" shouted his mom.

"Well, look at that," said his dad.

"Forsooth, Sir Rob, you're famous!" said Charlie. "Dare ye mingle with the dastardly likes of us?"

"Yeah," said Robert. It was okay for

Charlie to tease. He was still working on his Middle Ages project, and he talked like that, even at the dinner table. It was like eating with King Arthur, except King Arthur probably never had a buzz cut.

Finally, Robert's mom and Charlie went back to what they were doing. Robert was about to go upstairs when his dad shouted, "What's wrong with people?"

Robert stopped. He thought his dad was talking to him, but when he turned around, he saw his dad was still watching the news. A reporter asked a girl why she wore a ring in her nose. The girl squinted into the camera. "Everybody wears them," she said. "It's the fashion."

"How can anyone be so stupid?" said Robert's dad. "Nobody thinks for themselves anymore. Surely not every girl wants to put a hole in her nose and look like a pig." Robert saw the little vein in his father's neck jump.

Robert didn't think he should leave while his father was yelling about nose rings, even if it had nothing to do with him.

His dad noticed that he was still there.

"Robert, would you wear a ring in your nose if someone told you to?"

"No," said Robert. For one thing, his parents would kill him if he did. For another, how would you blow your nose? Didn't it hurt? No, he definitely would not put a ring through his nose.

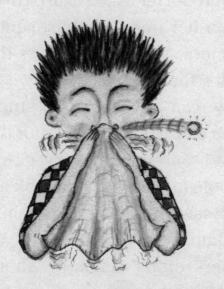

"This is what I was trying to tell you about those fancy sneakers, Tiger. It's the same thing. Lemming behavior."

"What's lemming behavior?" asked Robert. He knew there was no point trying to explain any more about the sneakers.

"Lemmings are little mouselike rodents," said his father. "They follow a leader blindly and don't think for themselves. If the leader jumps into the river and drowns, the rest will follow him."

Well, that *is* kind of what happened with the sneaker snobs at school, thought Robert. If only his dad could understand that he wasn't really like that.

Robert looked down at his blistered feet. Or was he?

Bigfoot

The next morning, Robert decided he would show the sneaker snobs at school that he was no lemming. But when he tried to put his new sneakers on, he discovered he couldn't get them on his feet. His toes were still blistered and sore from the hiking boots. What could he do? He needed shoes, but they had to be big enough not to press on his toes.

Charlie had left for school. Robert sneaked into his brother's room and looked in his closet. He found a cardboard shield and a breastplate and helmet covered with aluminum foil that Charlie had made for his presentation on the Middle Ages. In the back, he found a pair of basketball sneakers. They seemed way too big, but Robert took them.

In his room, he stuffed a sock into the toe of each sneaker. Then he put on his thickest socks. He slipped on the sneakers and tied the laces as tight as he could. The shoes were still too big and slipped up and down, but at least he could get them on his feet.

Robert picked up his book bag and started for the stairs. *Thunk!* He had tripped over his own feet. He picked himself up. He had to slow down.

Therump-bump. Therump-bump. Therump-bump. He went down the stairs slowly. His dad and Charlie were already gone. His mom was finishing her coffee. He had to make

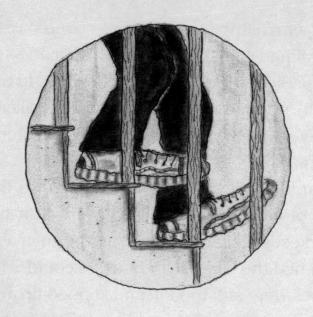

sure his mom did not see his feet or she might make him change his shoes. That would be too painful. He carried his book bag low to the ground, hoping it would hide his feet. He slid onto his chair at the table and drank his orange juice.

When his mom got up to put her cup in the dishwasher, Robert got up, too. He lifted his feet high so he wouldn't trip. At the front door, he shouted, "Bye, Mom!"

"So long, Rob," his mom called from the kitchen.

Robert carefully stepped outside and went down the two front steps.

He couldn't walk to school this way, so, once again, he got on the bus. "Hi, Robert," said Vanessa Nicolini. Luckily, she couldn't see his feet from where she sat.

"Hi," Robert answered. He found a seat halfway back in the bus and looked out the window. At Paul's corner, he called to him to get on the bus.

"So are we taking the bus all the time now?" asked Paul, sliding into the seat next to him.

"No, just this one more time. Look." Robert pointed down at his feet.

"No way!" cried Paul. "Those are not your real feet."

"They're Charlie's basketball sneakers. I had to borrow them. My feet would not go into my new sneakers."

Paul looked at him funny. "Are you sure you want to do this? How can you walk in those things?"

"Slowly, that's how," said Robert. "I have to do it. I can't go barefoot."

Paul shrugged. "Okay. If you say so."

Robert was the last one off the bus when they got to school. Everything was fine until he was almost in the classroom.

Jesse came running up to him, out of breath. "Robert, what are those ridiculous things on your feet?" He laughed so loudly that other kids turned around. They laughed, too.

"Man, look at those clown feet!"

"Hey, Bigfoot is visiting our school!"

"Robert, how did your feet grow like that?"

Robert didn't answer anyone. He just hurried inside to his seat and tried to keep his feet out of view.

By lunchtime, Robert was tired of clomping around and having everyone laugh at him. He took off Charlie's sneakers, tied them together, and slung them over his shoulder. He would just walk around in his sock feet the rest of the day.

"Robert, is something wrong?" Mrs. Bernthal asked him.

"No."

"Well, why don't you put your shoes on?"

"I can't," said Robert.

"Why not?"

"I have a foot disease."

"What kind of foot disease?" asked Mrs. Bernthal, concerned.

"Um . . . it's called . . . burning toes disease."

"Really?" said Mrs. Bernthal. "I'm sorry to hear that." She wrote something quickly on a notepad. "Here. Take this to Nurse Noonan right away."

Nurse Noonan! Robert gulped. She was as big as a bear and never smiled. Nobody knew what she did to kids who were sent to her. Nobody in Mrs. Bernthal's class had ever gone to Nurse Noonan's office.

He took the note and the pass and left the room. Nobody made a sound. When the door closed behind him, Robert felt a shiver go up his spine.

Nurse Noonan

Padding down the hall to Nurse Noonan's office, Robert could hardly breathe. What was he in for now? He never should have listened to Jesse. Who was Jesse, anyway—the fashion police? All of this happened because he'd followed the crowd, just like a lemming.

At the door to the nurse's office, he listened. There were no sounds coming from inside. Maybe she was not in! He knocked lightly.

"Come in," answered a strong voice. Robert gulped and opened the door slowly. There was a huge woman standing by the medicine cabinet staring at him. She was dressed in white pants and a white top. Her hair was white, too, like a fuzzy cap. She looked like a bear, all right. A polar bear.

"Well, and what's wrong with you?" she boomed.

Robert opened his mouth and nothing came out.

"Speak up, son. What's your trouble? Have a tummy ache? Sore throat? What is it?"

"My . . . feet." Robert stared down at his sock feet.

"Where are your shoes?" Nurse Noonan asked.

"I left them in my classroom."

Nurse Noonan had Robert sit down and take off his socks.

"Oh, my!" she said, looking at his red toes with the blisters. "What in the world did this to your feet?"

"I . . . I wore boots that were too small," he said.

Nurse Noonan stood up tall. "Tell your mother it's time to get you shoes that fit!" Her voice almost rocked Robert off the chair.

The large woman went to the medicine cabinet and took down a bottle and some cotton balls. She dabbed at Robert's toes with the medicine. His toes felt a lot better already. Nurse Noonan put Band-Aids on two toes.

"Keep your shoes off until the end of the day. You can walk around in your socks. You'll have to put your shoes on to go outside, but the Band-Aids will help. And when you get home, throw those shoes away. Do you hear me?"

"Yes, ma'am." Robert put his socks back on.

As he was leaving, he turned around. "Um . . . Nurse Noonan?"

"Yes, what is it?"

"My mother didn't know I wore those boots. She just bought me new sneakers."

Nurse Noonan pushed her glasses down her nose and looked over them. "Well, why on earth would you wear those boots, then?"

Robert didn't know how to answer her. It sounded so foolish. He just shrugged. "I don't know," he said.

"Well, I guess you won't be wearing them again. Right?"

Robert forced a weak smile. "Right." He opened the door and left.

Nurse Noonan wasn't so bad. She was huge, and her voice was scary, but she was pretty nice. And she had made his feet feel a lot better.

When Robert returned to his class-room, everyone stopped what they were doing to look at him. "He's okay," someone whispered.

"Yo, Robert!" called Lester Willis.

Mrs. Bernthal interrupted the class. "Robert, take your seat. We're in the middle of spelling. Open your book to page thirty-four."

Robert slid into his chair and opened his spelling book. He and Paul looked at each other. He would tell Paul on the way home about Nurse Noonan. But he wouldn't tell anyone else. Let them think whatever they wanted. Maybe it would make up for their laughing at him.

Sea Turtles

By Monday, Robert's blisters were healing. His mom had put more medicine on them. He could wear his new sneakers again. At last he could show everyone he was not a lemming.

Before Robert could sit at his table, Jesse was in his face. "So, you're back to those," said Jesse, looking at Robert's feet.

"Yup. I am," said Robert. "I like these sneakers." He slid his books onto the shelf under the table.

"I think they're nice," said Susanne Lee. Robert looked up. The surprise on

Jesse's face almost made him laugh. There was a giggle behind Robert. It was Vanessa. She must have thought it was funny, too. And even Susanne Lee seemed to be on his side now.

Robert felt so good that he volunteered to be first when they gave their reports. His report was on sea turtles. Ever since Frank Farraday said he was going to study them this summer, Robert had tried to find out all he could about them.

Robert loved the big goofy-looking creatures. He saw a lot of pictures of them in the books he read. But the more he read about them, the more upset he became. These wonderful creatures were dying all over the place. Frank Farraday was right. They were disappearing. And it was all because of people. Pretty soon after he'd started reading about the sea turtles, Robert knew that's what his report would be about. And now he was ready.

He began. "Sea turtles live in oceans all over the world." Robert took a string out of his pocket. He taped one end of the string to Mrs. Bernthal's desk and stretched the string out, holding the other end in his hand. "That's six feet," he said. "Some sea turtles grow six feet long." Everyone stretched their necks to see. "There used to be a lot more of them, but they are dying because of things people do." He unfolded a piece of notebook paper and read:

"People steal turtle eggs and eat them.

"They put up bright lights on beaches, where turtles lay their eggs. When baby turtles hatch and leave their nests, they are confused by the lights and crawl toward them instead of into the ocean, and they die.

"People kill turtles to make stuff out of them, like combs.

"They catch them in their nets when they fish for shrimp.

"They leave garbage on beaches that can be washed into the ocean, or they throw things off their boats. Turtles get tangled in the plastic rings that come around six-packs of soda. Or they eat plastic bags, because they look just like jellyfish floating in the water. If a turtle swallows a plastic bag, it could die."

Robert stopped for a breath.

"I don't know how to fix the whole problem. There are people studying what to do about it. But I think I know how I can help. And how all kids can."

"Well, good, Robert. Let's hear it," said Mrs. Bernthal.

"Never throw any garbage into the water. Not even a candy wrapper. Cut up the plastic rings from soda six-packs. And you know those balloons you buy in the park, or have at parties? With helium in them?"

"Yes, go on."

"Kids should never let them go up into the sky."

"Why not?"

"Because when they come down they could go into the ocean, and if sea turtles see them they'll think they're jellyfish, just like with plastic bags. And they'll eat them and die."

"We're not near the ocean," said Matt Blakey.

"Ah, but we have lakes and rivers, and they lead to the ocean," said Mrs. Bernthal. "Right, Robert?"

Robert nodded.

"You did an excellent job, Robert. I didn't know that about balloons," said Mrs. Bernthal. "Class, that's a very good idea." She went to the chalkboard and wrote:

NEVER LET A BALLOON FLY UP INTO THE AIR.

As Robert took his seat, Paul gave him a high five. That's when he really knew he had done a good job.

Emily Asher spoke next about rain forests. Robert settled back in his seat.

At recess, Susanne Lee Rodgers came up to Robert and told him he'd done a great report. "I will never let a balloon go again," she promised.

Vanessa Nicolini wrote him a note with a heart on it. It said, "I hope your feet are better." Robert looked her way and smiled. Vanessa giggled.

As soon as he had stood up to Jesse, nobody said anything more about his sneakers. The sneaker snobs had finally left him alone.

That night at dinner, Robert told everyone the whole story. About the sneakers, and Frank Farraday, and Nurse Noonan, and sea turtles. Everyone had something to say.

"Tiger, you make me proud," said his father. "I'm so glad you didn't let other people make up your mind for you."

"And what an interesting idea you had about the balloons," said his mother. "Very clever."

Charlie didn't say anything. He got up and ran out of the room.

"What's wrong with Charlie?" asked Robert's dad.

"I don't know," said his mom.

Suddenly, Charlie came marching in, wearing his aluminum foil armor and carrying a sneaker on a broom handle.

"What are you doing?" said Robert.

"Here's your banner, Sir Rob," Charlie said, parading around the table. "You've won the battle against the sneaker snobs!"

Charlie made a great knight. Everyone laughed at his performance. Even Robert's feet were happy. He tapped his sneakers together under the table as he helped himself to another taco.